Mr. Griz

Shaw's

SOLO

by Bryan Patrick Avery   illustrated by Arief Putra

PICTURE WINDOW BOOKS
a capstone imprint

Published by Picture Window Books, an imprint of Capstone.
1710 Roe Crest Drive
North Mankato, Minnesota 56003
capstonepub.com

Library of Congress Cataloging-in-Publication Data
Names: Avery, Bryan Patrick, author. | Putra, Arief, illustrator.
Title: Shaw's solo / by Bryan Patrick Avery ; illustrated by
Arief Putra.
Description: North Mankato, Minnesota : Picture Window Books,
an imprint of Capstone, [2022] | Series: Mr. Grizley's class |
Audience: Ages 5–7. | Audience: Grades K–1. | Summary: Shaw
loves to sing and dreams of becoming a star but when he is
asked to perform a solo for the mayor he needs the help of his
classmates to overcome his nervousness and sing.
Identifiers: LCCN 2021006150 (print) | LCCN 2021006151
(ebook) | ISBN 9781663910301 (hardcover) | ISBN
9781663920980 (paperback) | ISBN 9781663910271 (pdf) |
ISBN 9781663910295 (kindle edition)
Subjects: LCSH: Singing—Juvenile fiction. | Confidence—
Juvenile fiction. | Helping behavior—Juvenile fiction. |
Friendship—Juvenile fiction. | CYAC: Anxiety—Fiction. |
Singing—Fiction. | Schools—Fiction.
Classification: LCC PZ7.1.A9736 Sh 2021 (print) | LCC
PZ7.1.A9736 (ebook) | DDC 813.6 [E]—dc23
LC record available at https://lccn.loc.gov/2021006150
LC ebook record available at https://lccn.loc.gov/2021006151

Designed by Kay Fraser and Dina Her

TABLE OF CONTENTS

Chapter 1
The Stomach Pain...........................**7**

Chapter 2
The Recess Solution **13**

Chapter 3
The Big Moment...........................**20**

Mr. Grizley's Class ★

Cecilia Gomez

Shaw Quinn

Emily Kim

Mordecai Foster

Nathan Wu

Ashok Aparnam

Ryan Clayborn

Rahma Abdi

Nicole Washington

Alijah Wilson

Suddha Agarwal

Chad Werner

Semira Madani

Pierre Boucher

Zoe Charmichael

Dmitry Orloff

Camila Jennings

Madison Tanaka

Annie Barberra

Bobby Lewis

CHAPTER 1

The Stomach Pain

Shaw sat at his desk. He held his stomach and groaned.

"Are you okay?" Zoe asked.

Shaw finished the last math problem on his worksheet. He put his pencil down.

"It's my stomach," he said. "I don't think I can sing today."

Mr. Grizley looked up
from his desk. "I hear a lot
of talking," he said. "What's
going on?"

"Can I go to the nurse's
office?" Shaw asked. "I don't
feel so good."

Mr. Grizley went to speak to Shaw. "What's wrong?" he asked.

"His stomach hurts," Zoe explained.

Shaw nodded.

"I'm supposed to sing in front of the mayor and the whole school today," Shaw said. "I don't think I can do it. I'm too nervous."

"That's normal," Mr. Grizley said. "Everybody gets nervous at one time or another."

"Even you?" Shaw asked.

"Even me," Mr. Grizley said.

The bell rang for recess.

"Go to recess and have some fun," Mr. Grizley told Shaw. "That might help you feel better."

CHAPTER 2

The Recess Solution

Shaw followed his friends out to recess.

"I don't think I'm ever going to feel better," he said.

Shaw's friends tried to help calm his nerves.

"Let's play tag," Bobby said.

Mordecai tapped Shaw on the arm.

"You're it!" Mordecai shouted. He and Bobby ran away.

Shaw chased Bobby and Mordecai around the playground.

They sprinted past the swings. They raced around the basketball courts. They dashed across the soccer field.

Then, they flopped down
on a bench to rest.

"My stomach still feels
funny," Shaw said.

"Before my magic shows," Mordecai said, "I close my eyes and imagine giving the best performance I can. It always helps me."

Shaw closed his eyes. He imagined singing for the mayor.

His voice cracked. He forgot the words. Everyone laughed.

Shaw's stomach started to feel worse.

"It's my dream to be a famous singer," he said. "But I can't even sing in front of my own school."

Zoe and Emily rushed over to the bench.

"Hey, Shaw," Emily said. "We have something that might help."

CHAPTER 3

The Big Moment

Zoe held up a small bottle. It was filled with glitter.

"It's a meditation bottle," she said.

She turned the bottle upside down. The glitter floated to the bottom.

"That's cool!" Shaw said.

"I use it whenever I need to relax," Emily explained.

Zoe gave Shaw the bottle.

Shaw turned the bottle over. He took deep breaths. The glitter drifted down.

Shaw smiled.

"Hey, it worked!" he said. "I do feel better."

Right before it was time for Shaw to sing, he used the meditation bottle again. Then, he walked onto the stage.

Shaw held the microphone.
The mayor sat in the front row.
Shaw saw his class behind her.

The music started, and Shaw
began to sing.

He didn't feel nervous anymore. He just felt happy to be doing something he loved.

When Shaw finished singing, the mayor jumped to her feet and clapped.

"Bravo!" she cheered.

Later, Shaw posed for a picture with the mayor and Mr. Grizley.

"You were wonderful!" the mayor told Shaw. "I would have been so nervous."

"Oh, everyone gets nervous sometimes," Shaw said. He smiled at Mr. Grizley. "Even me."

LET'S MAKE A MEDITATION BOTTLE

- 1 small clear bottle with a top
- liquid dish soap
- warm water
- glitter in your favorite colors

WHAT YOU DO:
1. Pour enough liquid dish soap into the bottle or jar to fill it a quarter full.

2. Fill the bottle the rest of the way with warm water. Leave a little room at the top for glitter.

3. Put the top on the bottle and shake it to mix the soap and water. You may get a little foam. That's okay.

4. Open the glitter and pour some into the bottle. Cover and shake to mix it.

That's it! Your bottle is ready. Whenever you want to relax or calm down, grab your bottle and turn it upside down. Take deep breaths and focus on the glitter as it tumbles and swirls its way to the bottom of the bottle.

GLOSSARY

famous (FAY-muhs)—very well known

meditation (med-ih-TAY-shuhn)—thinking deeply and quietly

microphone (MYE-kruh-fohn)—a device used to make sounds louder, such as a person's voice

nervous (NUR-vuhss)—being fearful or worried in a specific situation

performance (pur-FOR-muhnss)—music, acting, or other entertainment presented for a group of people

stomach (STUHM-uhk)—part of the body where food is digested

TALK ABOUT IT

1. Why was Shaw's stomach bothering him at the beginning of the story? How does your body feel when you're nervous?

2. Have you ever been nervous about something? What did you do?

3. How did Shaw's friends try to help? What would you have suggested to Shaw?

WRITE ABOUT IT

1. Singing was Shaw's dream. Write a paragraph about your biggest dream.

2. Pretend you are a reporter and write a story about the mayor's visit to the school.

3. What song do you think Shaw sang for the mayor? What makes it a good choice?

ABOUT THE AUTHOR

Bryan Patrick Avery discovered his love of reading and writing at an early age when he received his first Bobbsey Twins mystery. He writes picture books, chapter books, middle grade, and graphic novels. He is the author of the picture book *The Freeman Field Photograph*, as well as "The Magic Day Mystery" in *Super Puzzletastic Mysteries*. Bryan lives in northern California with his family.

ABOUT THE ILLUSTRATOR

Arief Putra loves working and drawing in his home studio at the corner of Yogyakarta city in Indonesia. He enjoys coffee, cooking, space documentaries, and solving the Rubik's Cube. Living in a small house in a rural area with his wife and two sons, Arief has a big dream to spread positivity around the world through his art.